There's a Lion on the Dance Floor

By Kristin Harkison Paulus

Illustrations by Kelly Beroske

AuthorHouse™
1663 Liberty Drive
Bloomington, IN 47403
www.authorhouse.com
Phone: 1-800-839-8640

First published by AuthorHouse 3/11/2010

ISBN: 978-1-4490-2692-9 (sc)

Library of Congress Control Number: 2010900195

Printed in the United States of America
Bloomington, Indiana

This book is printed on acid-free paper.

authorHOUSE®

For Lauren, Zachary and Ryan who have made my life richer,
and inspired me with gifts of imagination, love and laughter.
- K.H.P.

For Mom, a woman who has always encouraged me to take chances.
- K.B.

A special thanks to our editors,
Dr. Philip J. Cotrell and Shena Vasko

There's a lion on the dance floor.
You'll never believe!

It's a party for people,
but *this* wildcat won't leave.

He's cutting
a rug,

doing
a jig,

jumping and bouncing,

and boy is he BIG!

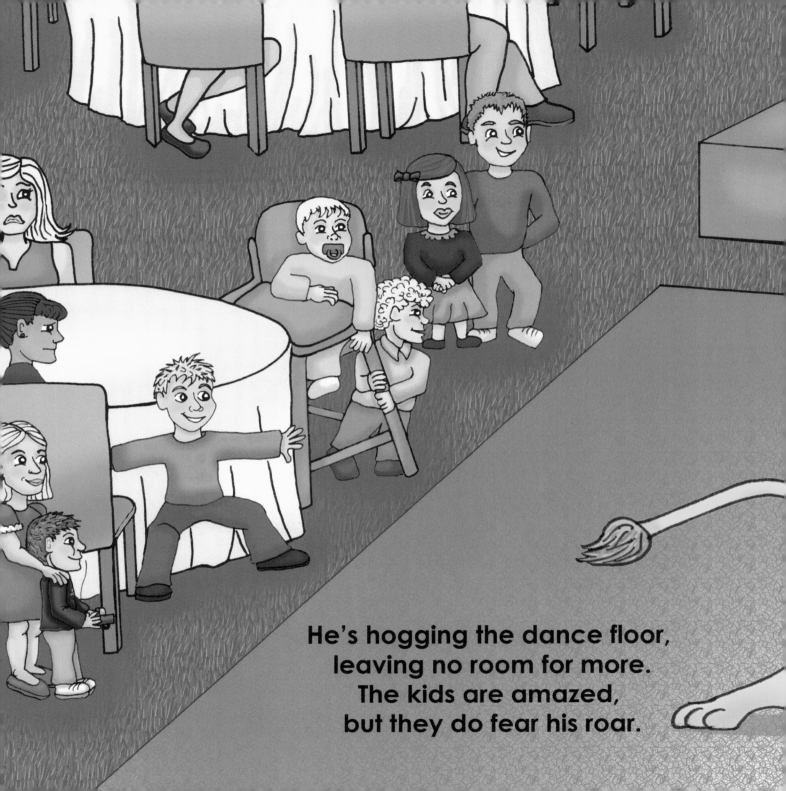

He's hogging the dance floor,
leaving no room for more.
The kids are amazed,
but they do fear his roar.

Will it be loud?

Will he try to bite?

Will he just shimmy it up
for the night?

It's such a strange sight, his mane flopping around. He grooves with the beat, and he sure loves the sound.

He's up on hind legs, then down on all fours.

He seems rather friendly, but we're all too frightened. Who will get closer to this giant titan?

What if he pounces during a musical verse?

It's hard to imagine what might happen next.
Everyone wonders when he'll need a rest.

I would like to mention he's a wonderful dancer.
I have questions to ask him, and I'm looking for answers.

I'll have to be brave and join him out there.
I wish I had protection from a tiger or bear!

I'm moving in closer, sneaking right past his tail.
UH-OH! He sees me, and I think I might wail!

I am frozen like a statue, waiting with worry.
He's staring at me, oh, I wish he would scurry.

The grown-ups and kids
all stare in awe as he speaks
while politely raising his paw.

"I know I am big and a little bit scary,
but I'm really kind-natured so please do not worry.

Most lions don't dance so I know I seem strange,
but I'm a regular lion with a regular mane.

I live in the wild and have my own den.
I have many other animal friends.

None of them love to dance
like I do,

so I'm looking for friends
who might like it too.

I left the forest and followed
the music.

That's how I got here,
where I can move it
and groove it.

Dancing is the greatest
part of my day,

when I shake and shimmy
my worries away.

Thanks for your bravery and for talking to me.
I was feeling left out and a little bit lonely.

So come and join me. I'll try to make room.
Feel the beat, and feel the boom.

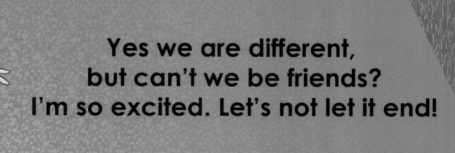

Yes we are different,
but can't we be friends?
I'm so excited. Let's not let it end!

Even though you are small and I'm very big,
let's dance, my new friend. Let's dance our own jig!"